# NOW I AM FOUR!

by Jane Belk Moncure

illustrated by Kathryn Hutton

created by **THE CHILD'S WORLD**

 CHILDRENS PRESS, CHICAGO

**Library of Congress Cataloging in Publication Data**

Moncure, Jane Belk.

  Now I am four.
  Summary: A child displays the many achievements of a
four-year-old.
  [1. Growth—Fiction]  I. Hutton, Kathryn, ill.
II. Title.
PZ7.M739Noh  1984          [E]          83-25270
ISBN 0-516-01878-7 (Childrens Press)

# NOW I AM FOUR!

Now that I am four,

I am growing
more and more.

Guess what?
I can lace my shoe . . .

and button up
my sweater too.

I can water my garden

and help it grow.

I can kick a football. . .

catch and throw!

I can build a city
with my blocks. . .

and make a grocery
store out of a box.

I can cut
and paste.

I can mix
and pour.

I can do lots of things,
now that I'm four.

I can play games. . .

I can swing very high. . .
and pretend I'm a
jet plane flying by.

I can climb into
my rocket ship. . .

18

then go down
the slide. . . and
pretend I'm an astronaut
taking a ride.

I like to make music.

I like to pretend.

I like to climb the
jungle gym. . .

# with a friend.

I like parties and clowns. . .

24

and pink lemonade.

I like elephants. . .

in a circus parade.

I like picture books. . .

and jumpy frogs. . .

I like bedtime stories
and puppy dogs.

Now that you are
four, how about you?
What do you like?
What can you do?